Baby Bear
goes
Camping

Lorette Broekstra

BRIMAX

D1261207

For my mother

First published in Great Britain in 2001 by Brimax
an imprint of Octopus Publishing Group Ltd
2-4 Heron Quays, London E14 4JP
UK, North American and South African licencee © Octopus Publishing Group Ltd
Text and illustrations © Lorette Broekstra 2001
Originally published in Australia 2001 by Thomas C. Lothian Pty Ltd
Isbn 1 8585 4408 4
Printed in Spain

All rights reserved. No part of this publication may be reproduced,
stored in a retrieval system, or transmitted in any form or by any means electronic,
mechanical, photocopying, recording or otherwise without the prior written
permission of the copyright holder.

t was an exciting day for Baby Bear.
He was going on his first camping trip.

He couldn't wait to start putting up
his very own tent.

After the tents were up and the beds were made
Papa Bear said, 'Let's go for a walk.'

On their walk Baby Bear said, 'Hello,' to an owl,

'Good afternoon,' to a frog,

'Hi,' to a bat

and, 'How do you do?' to a porcupine.

When they returned from their walk they were feeling
very hungry, so Papa Bear started a fire.

He cooked potatoes, carrots and green beans.
It was a delicious meal.

'Ah,' sighed Baby Bear, 'camping is good fun.'

'And very tiring.' He yawned.

It was bedtime for Baby Bear.
'Goodnight, Papa Bear.
Goodnight, Mama Bear,' said Baby Bear.

'Goodnight,' said Papa Bear.
'Sleep tight,' said Mama Bear.

But when Baby Bear got into bed he couldn't sleep.
There were too many strange noises.
'Whoo, whoo.' Baby Bear shivered.

'Ribbit! Ribbit!' Baby Bear shook.

And then he saw a huge shadow on
the side of his tent,

and another one on the other side!

Poor Baby Bear was feeling very scared.
He stumbled,

and started to fall.
'Ow!' said Baby Bear as he fell right out of the tent.

He looked up and saw Bat.
'Oh, it was you making that scary shadow!' he said.

Then he saw Porcupine.
'And it was you making that other shadow on my tent.'

'Whoo!' said Owl.

'Oh!' said Baby Bear. 'It was you making that sound.'

'Ribbit!'
'And that was you, Frog!'

'We just came to say goodnight to you, Baby Bear,'
said Bat, Porcupine, Owl and Frog.

Baby Bear laughed. 'Goodnight,' he said.

He went back into his tent,
climbed into his sleeping bag and had
his best sleep ever.